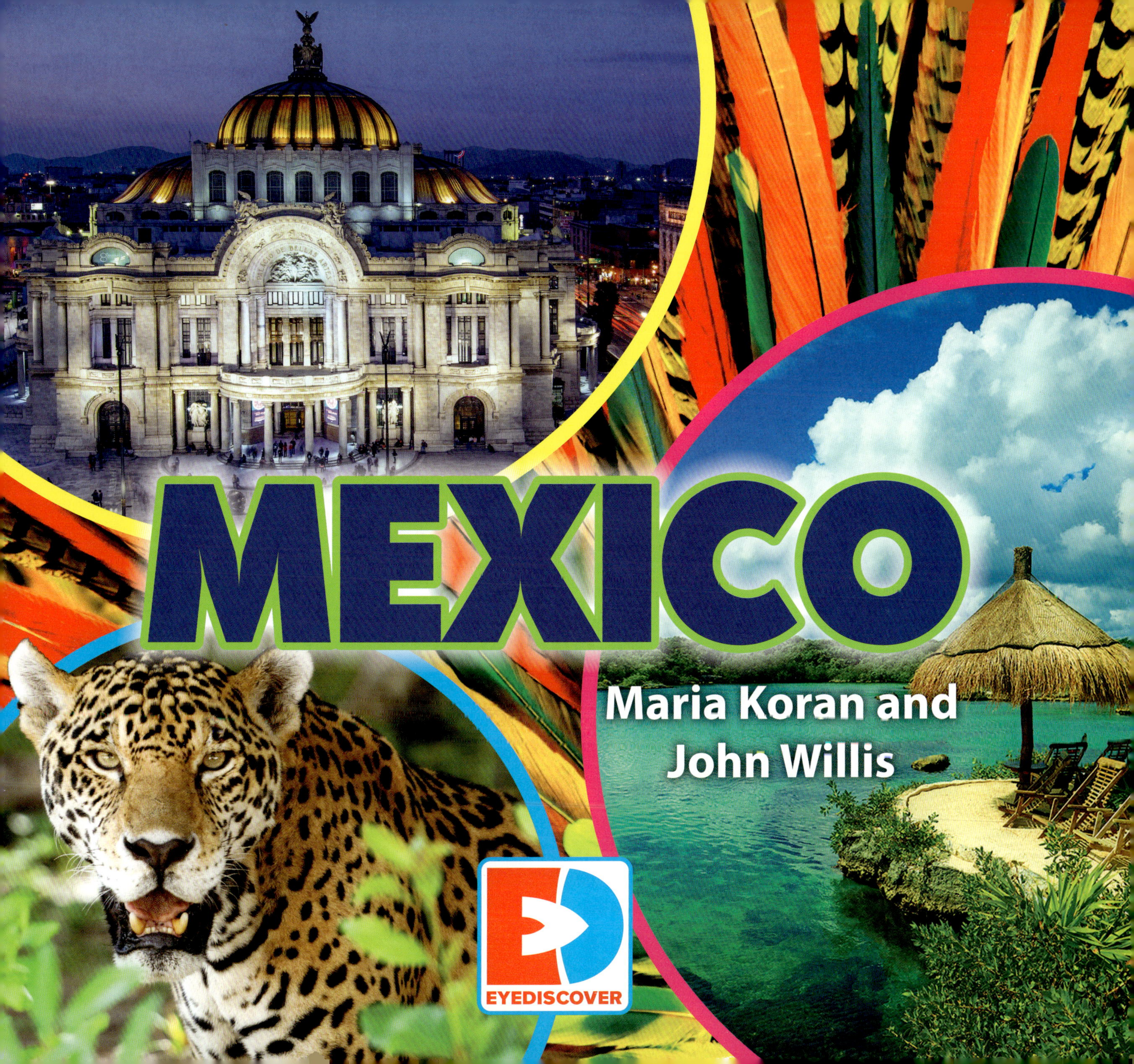

MEXICO

Maria Koran and John Willis

EYEDISCOVER

Go to **www.eyediscover.com** and enter this book's unique code.

BOOK CODE

AVU36539

EYEDISCOVER brings you optic readalongs that support active learning.

Published by AV2
276 5th Avenue, Suite 704 #917
New York, NY 10001
Website: www.eyediscover.com

Library of Congress Control Number: 2021937107

978-1-7911-4204-9 (hardcover)

Printed in Guangzhou, China
1 2 3 4 5 6 7 8 9 0 25 24 23 22 21

042021
102120

Project Coordinator: John Willis
Designer: Mandy Christiansen

The publisher acknowledges Getty Images, Alamy, and Shutterstock as the primary image suppliers for this title.

EYEDISCOVER provides enriched content, optimized for tablet use, that supplements and complements this book. EYEDISCOVER books strive to create inspired learning and engage young minds in a total learning experience.

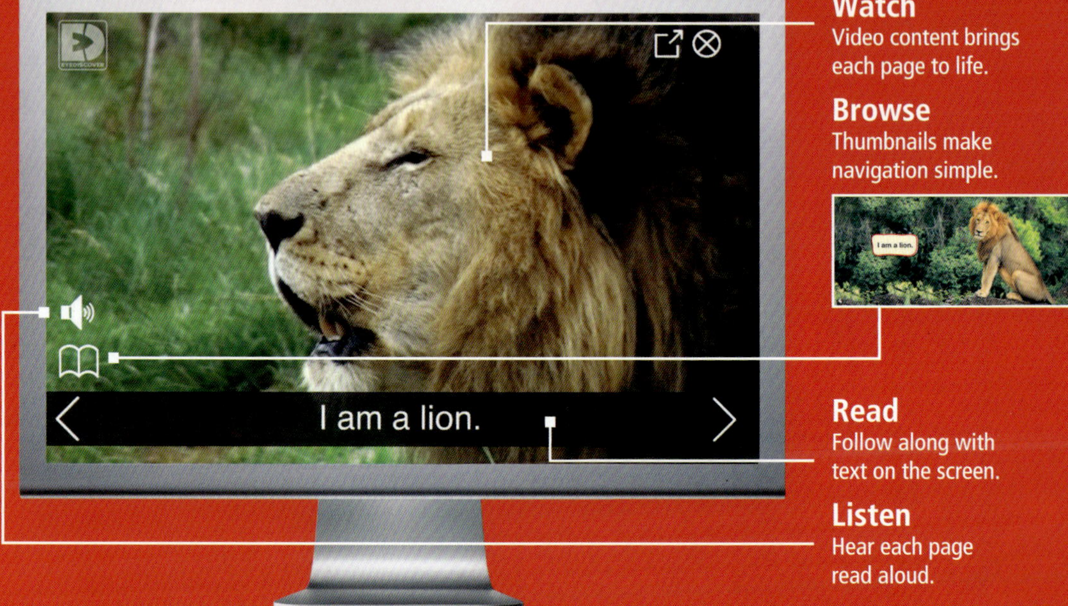

Watch
Video content brings each page to life.

Browse
Thumbnails make navigation simple.

Read
Follow along with text on the screen.

Listen
Hear each page read aloud.

Your EYEDISCOVER Optic Readalongs come alive with...

Audio
Listen to the entire book read aloud.

Video
High resolution videos turn each spread into an optic readalong.

OPTIMIZED FOR
- TABLETS
- WHITEBOARDS
- COMPUTERS
- AND MUCH MORE!

MEXICO

In this book, you will learn about

- where it is
- who lives there
- what it is known for

and much more!

Mexico is a country in North America.

2018
FORO INTERNACIONAL DE
MÚSICA NUEVA
MANUEL ENRIQUEZ
40
FIMNME
SEPTIEMBRE 21
- OCTUBRE 14
Palacio de
Bellas Artes

6

More than 125 million people live in Mexico.

Mexico City is the capital of Mexico. It is the oldest city in North America.

PALACIO DE BELLAS ARTES

Mexico is made up of 31 states. The state with the most people is named the State of Mexico.

UNO Y UNO
ALTO

Most people in Mexico speak Spanish. It is one of more than 60 languages in the country.

There are many symbols of Mexico. The Mexican flag is green, white, and red. It has an eagle in its center.

Animals can be symbols, too. The jaguar is Mexico's national mammal.

Mexico is one of the most visited countries in the world. People come to enjoy its beaches.

Mexico is also known for its history. Visitors can see buildings that were made long ago.

In **2019**, Mexico was the **7th most popular** country on Earth for **people to visit**.

A **jaguar** can **weigh more than 200 POUNDS** (91 kilograms).

The **world's biggest pyramid** is in **Mexico**. It was built more than **1,800 years** ago.

Mexico City

was founded about **500** years ago.

One of the first color televisions was **invented** in Mexico in **1940**.

More than **9 million** people **live** in **Mexico City**.

KEY WORDS

Research has shown that as much as 65 percent of all written material published in English is made up of 300 words. These 300 words cannot be taught using pictures or learned by sounding them out. They must be recognized by sight. This book contains 40 common sight words to help young readers improve their reading fluency and comprehension. This book also teaches young readers several important content words, such as proper nouns. These words are paired with pictures to aid in learning and improve understanding.

Page	Sight Words First Appearance
4	a, America, country, in, is
7	live, more, people, than
8	city, it, of, the
11	made, most, states, up, with
13	one
15	an, and, are, has, its, many, there, white
16	animals, be, can, too
19	come, to, world
20	also, for, long, see, that, were

Page	Content Words First Appearance
4	Mexico, North America
8	capital, Mexico City
11	State of Mexico
13	languages, Spanish
15	center, eagle, flag, symbols
16	jaguar, mammal
19	beaches
20	buildings, history, visitors

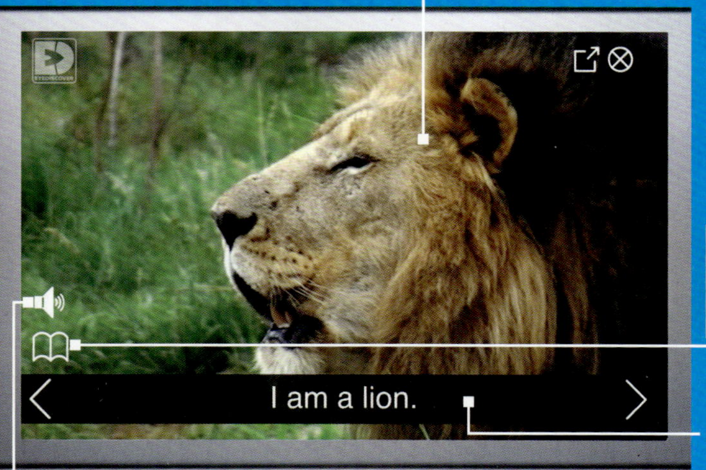

Watch
Video content brings each page to life.

Browse
Thumbnails make navigation simple.

Read
Follow along with text on the screen.

Listen
Hear each page read aloud.

Go to www.eyediscover.com and enter this book's unique code.

BOOK CODE

AVU36539